First Edition

ISBN-13: 978-1977632081
ISBN-10: 1977632084

For information about authoring or illustrating your own children's book, visit www.familyfables.org.

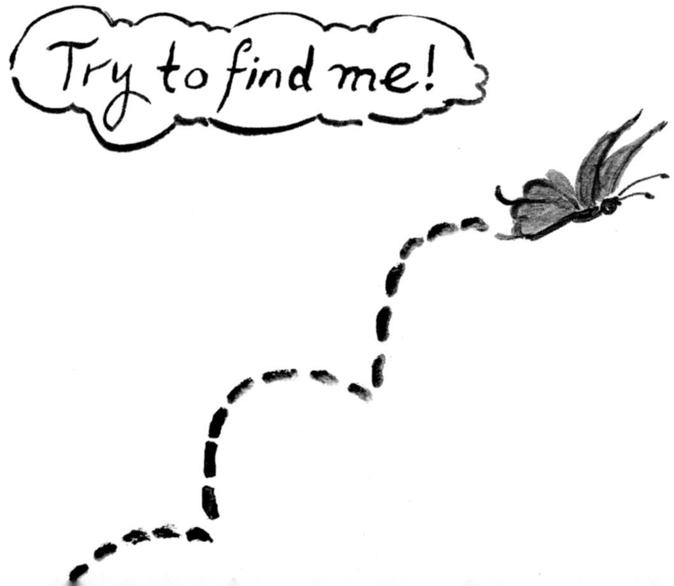
Try to find me!

Still Bailey had pride
For who was inside
But could not fit in
No matter how much she tried.

So, to trick the whole crew,
Bailey tried something new.
On Halloween day,
She slipped on a costume.

Bailey returned to the spot.
The frogs gave it no thought.
She blended in with them all
And was taught quite a lot.

She learned how to hop,
How to croak, how to plop,

How to swim, how to eat,
How to even belly flop.

By the end of the day,
It was quite easy to say
That this army of frogs
Had a new protégé.

Then to their surprise,
She shed her disguise.
They saw her paws, her fur,
And her puppy dog eyes.

"You tricked us, you dog.
Get out of our bog!
Like we've said all along,
A dog is no frog."

With that Bailey hopped,
She croaked, and she plopped,

She swam, and she ate,
And even belly flopped.

The frogs looked amazed.
Even awarded her praise.
For despite how she looked,
She was them in all ways.

So, the frogs learned their lesson
That it's not what you're dressed in;
It's who's inside that defines you.
Of that, there's no question.

Made in the USA
San Bernardino, CA
24 October 2017